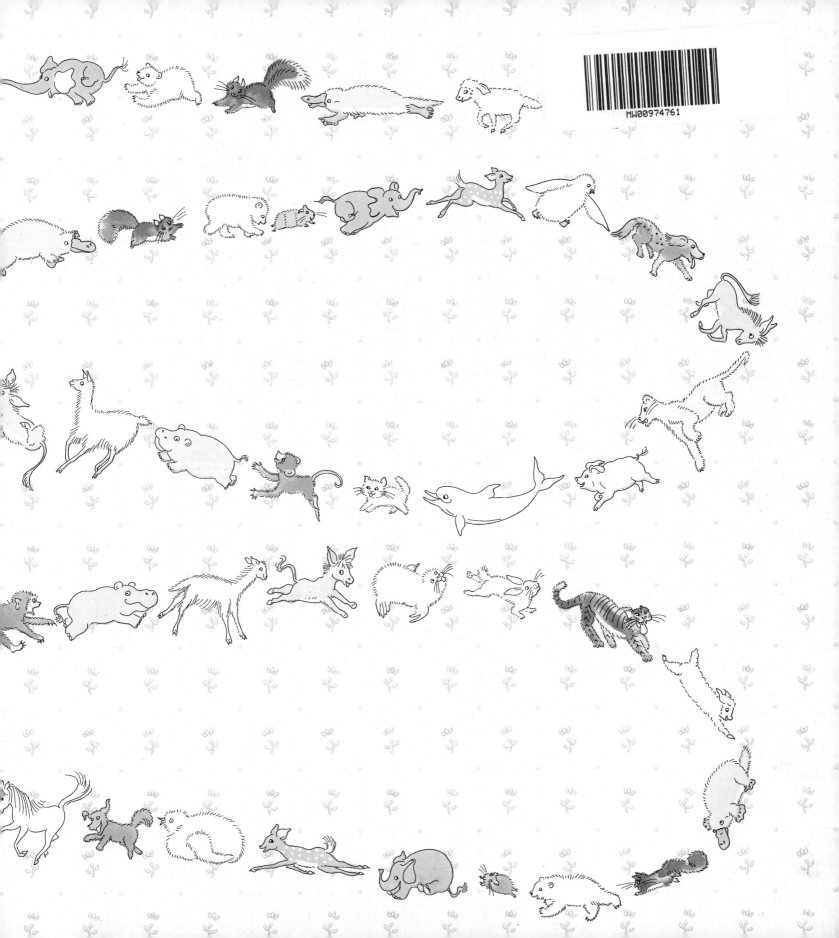

FIND DEMI'S

Can you find
this bunny
nibbling a carrot?

bunny

Grosset & Dunlap · New York

Copyright © 1990 by Demi. All rights reserved. Published by
Grosset & Dunlap, Inc., a member of The Putnam and Grosset Book Group, New York.
Published simultaneously in Canada. Printed in Singapore.
Library of Congress Catalog Card Number: 89-82234
ISBN 0-448-19169-5 A B C D E F G H I J

BABY ANIMALS

For
Elise Marie
Buedel

lamb

Can you find
this woolly lamb
sniffing a daisy?

tiger

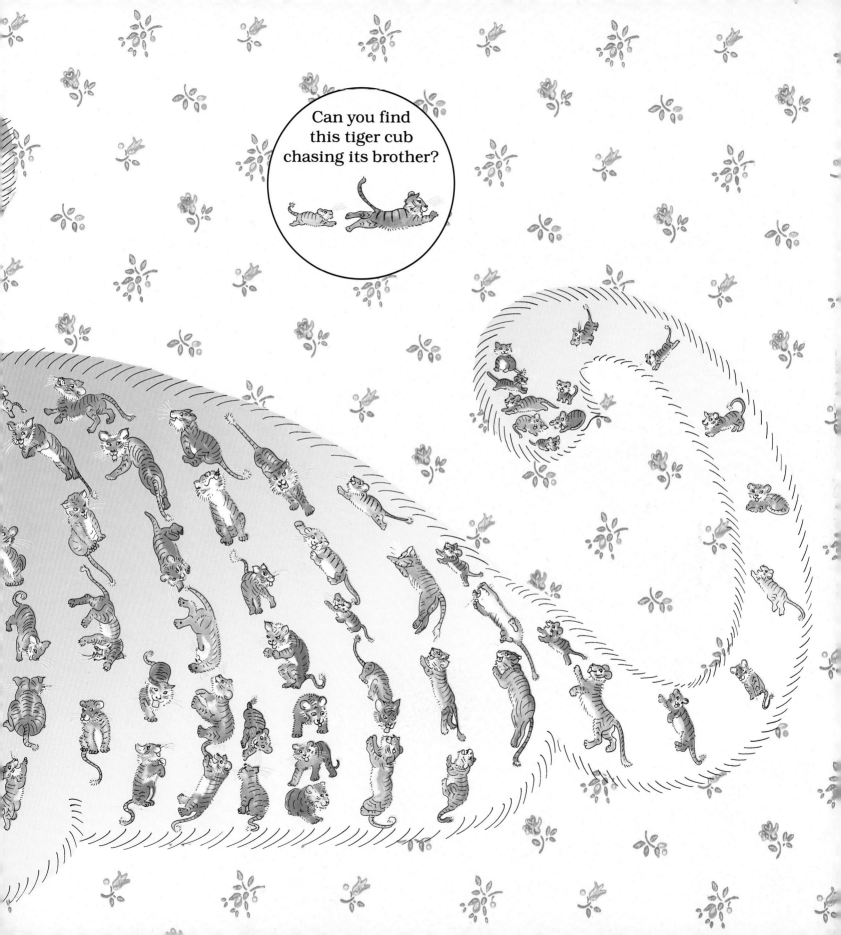

Can you find
this tiger cub
chasing its brother?

pony

Can you find
this pretty pony
with a yellow balloon?

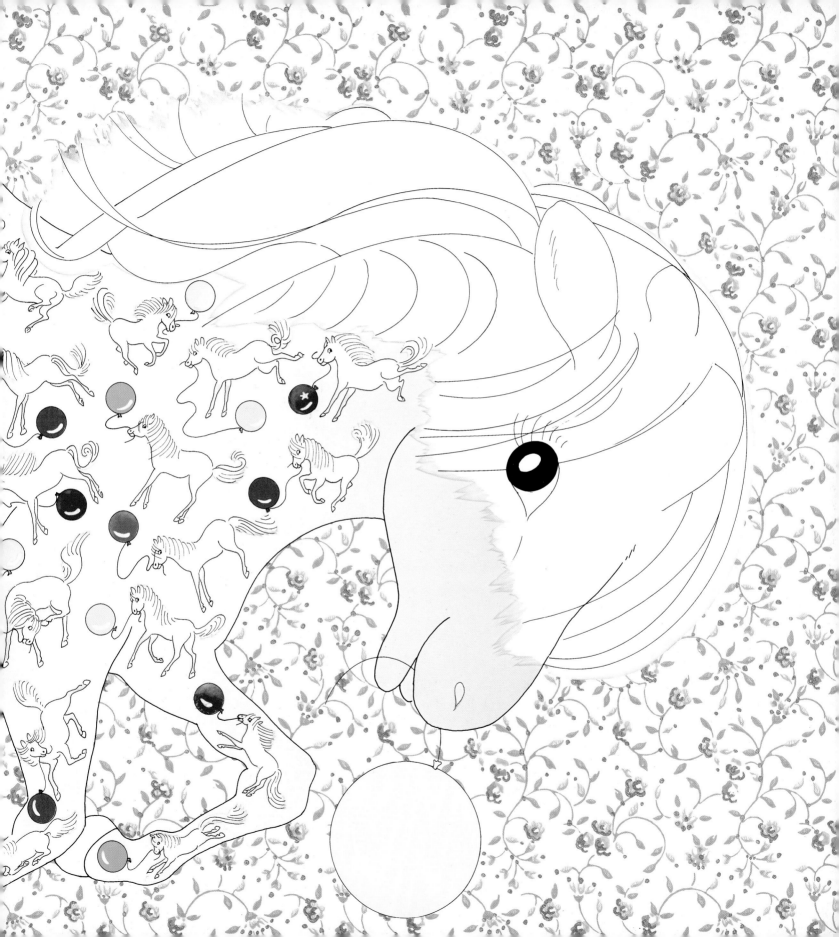

pig

Can you find this roly-poly piglet?

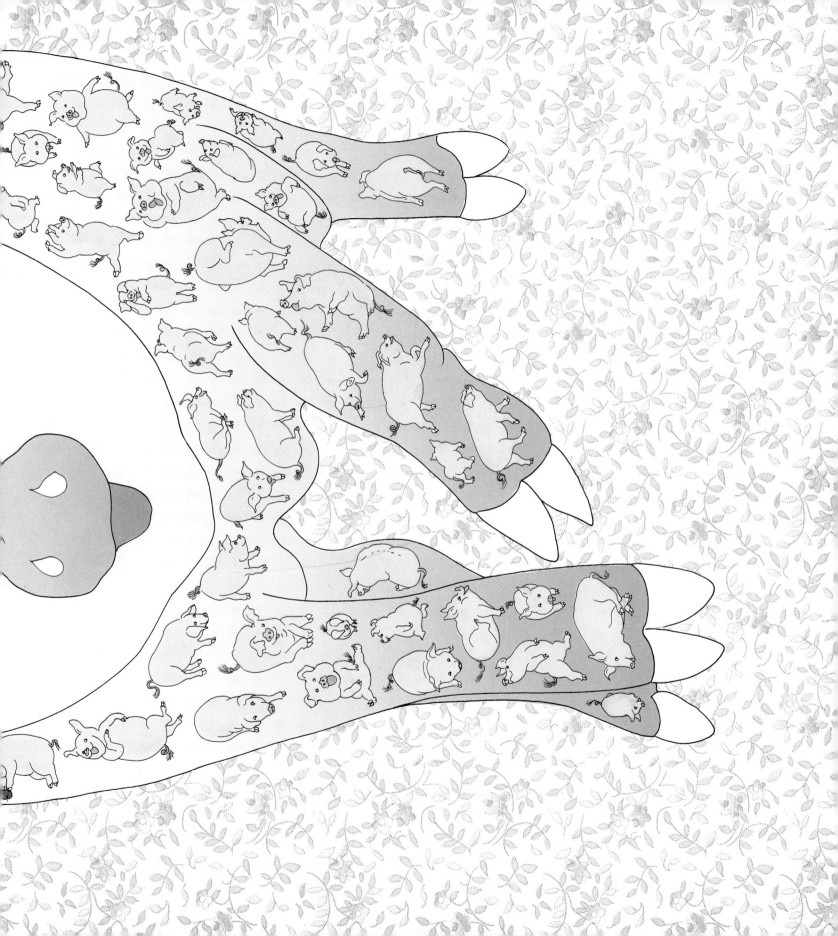

Can you find
this mother bear
feeding her cubs?

polar bear

guinea pigs

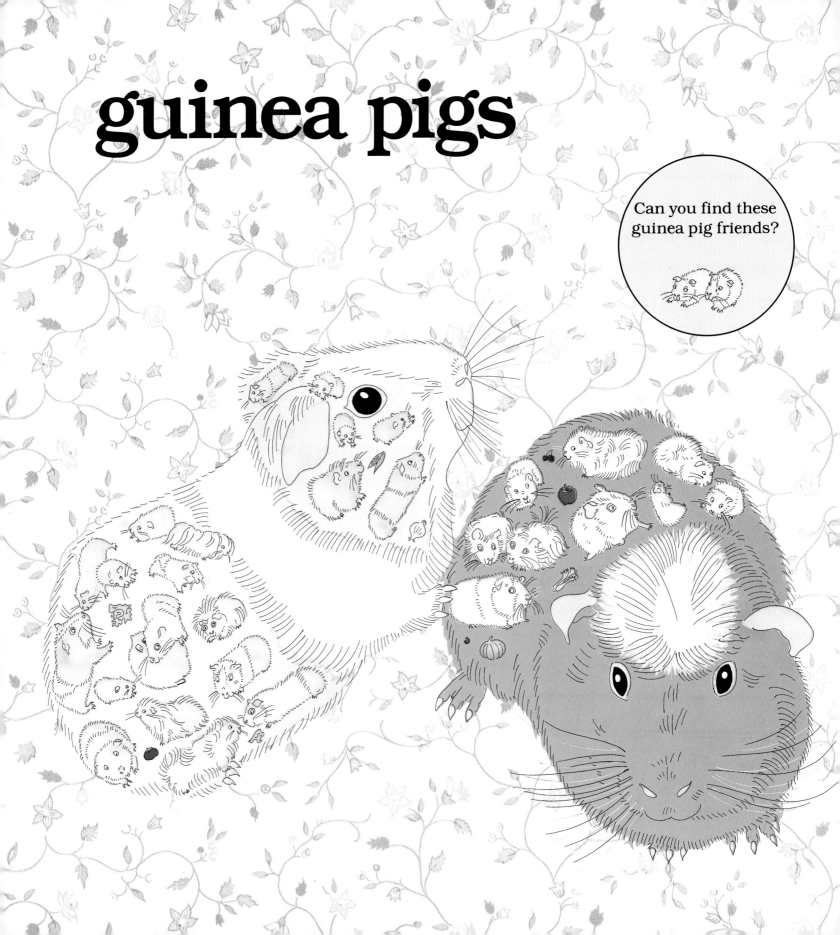

Can you find these guinea pig friends?

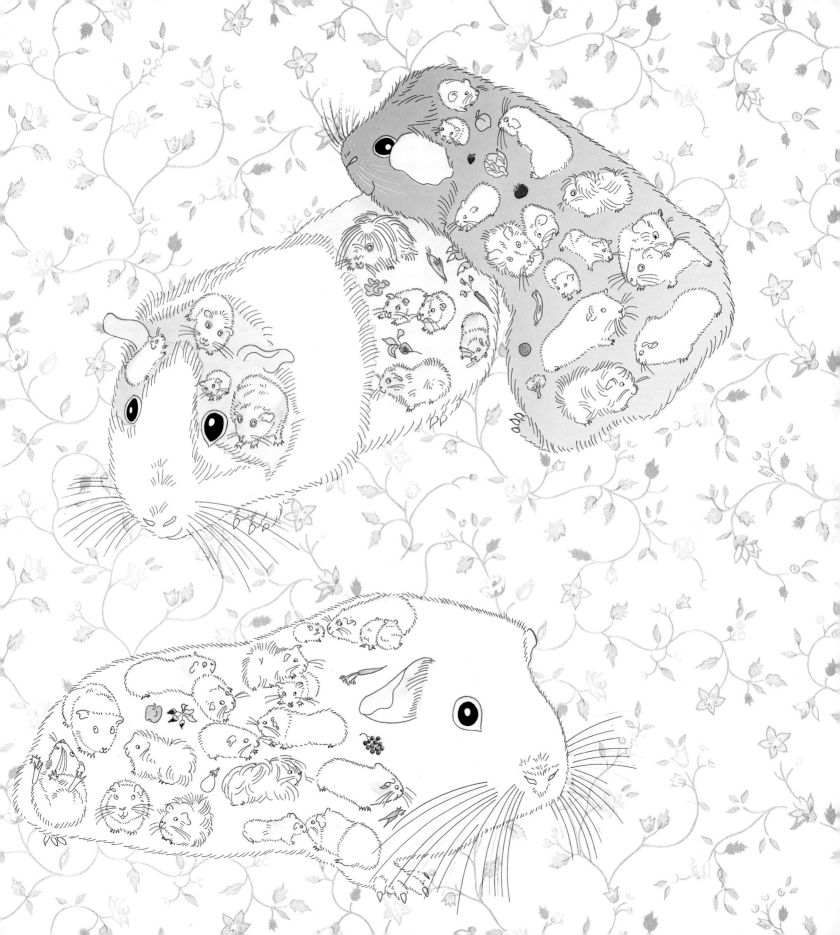

lion

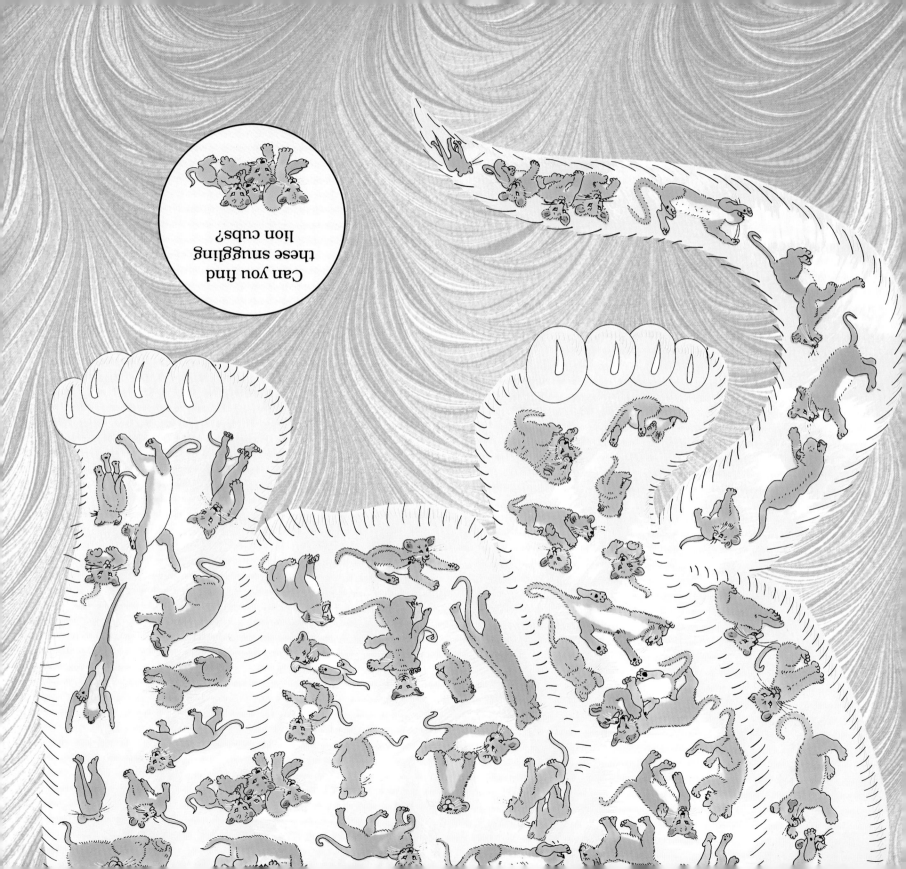

Can you find these snuggling lion cubs?

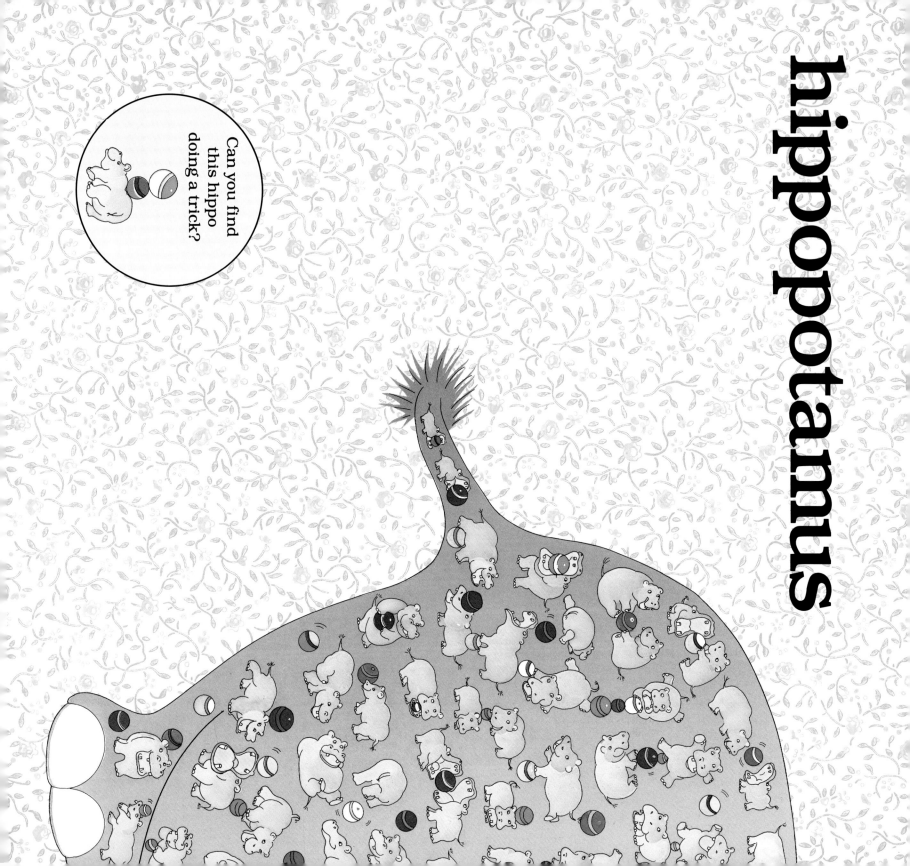

Can you find
this hippo
doing a trick?

hippopotamus

penguin

Can you find this fuzzy penguin chick?

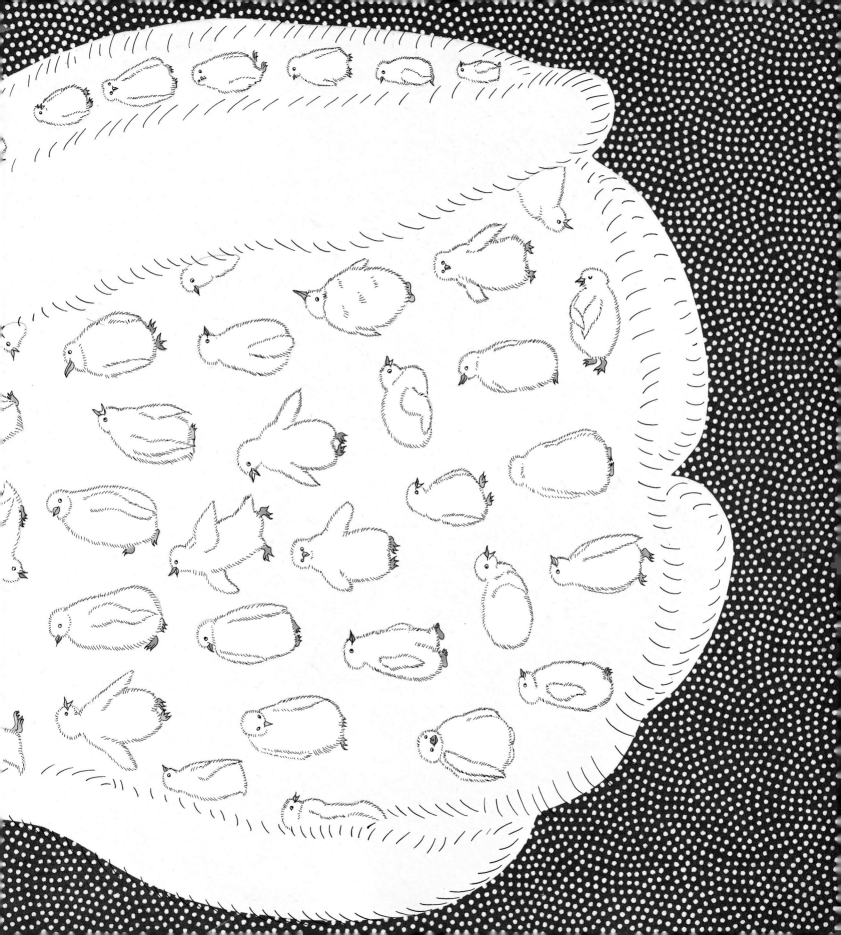

dolphin

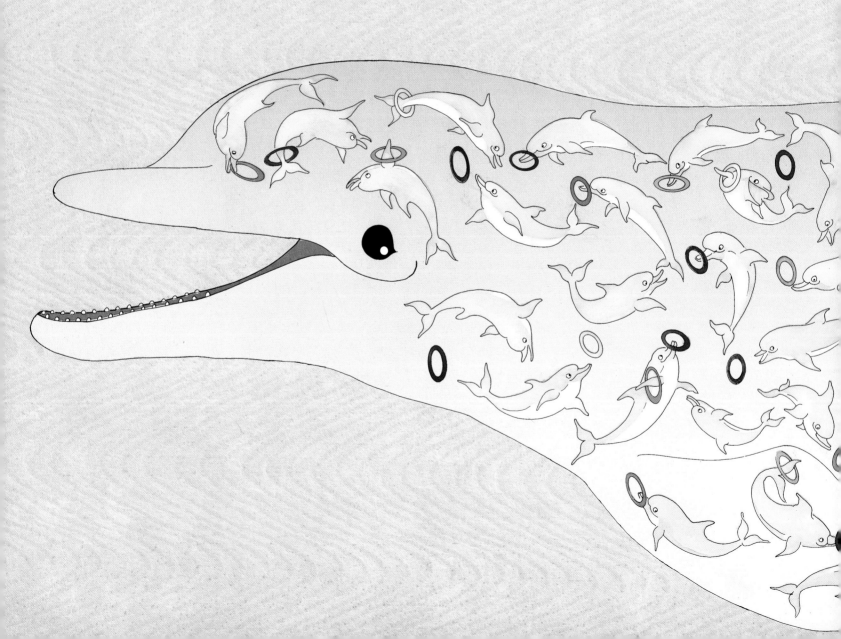

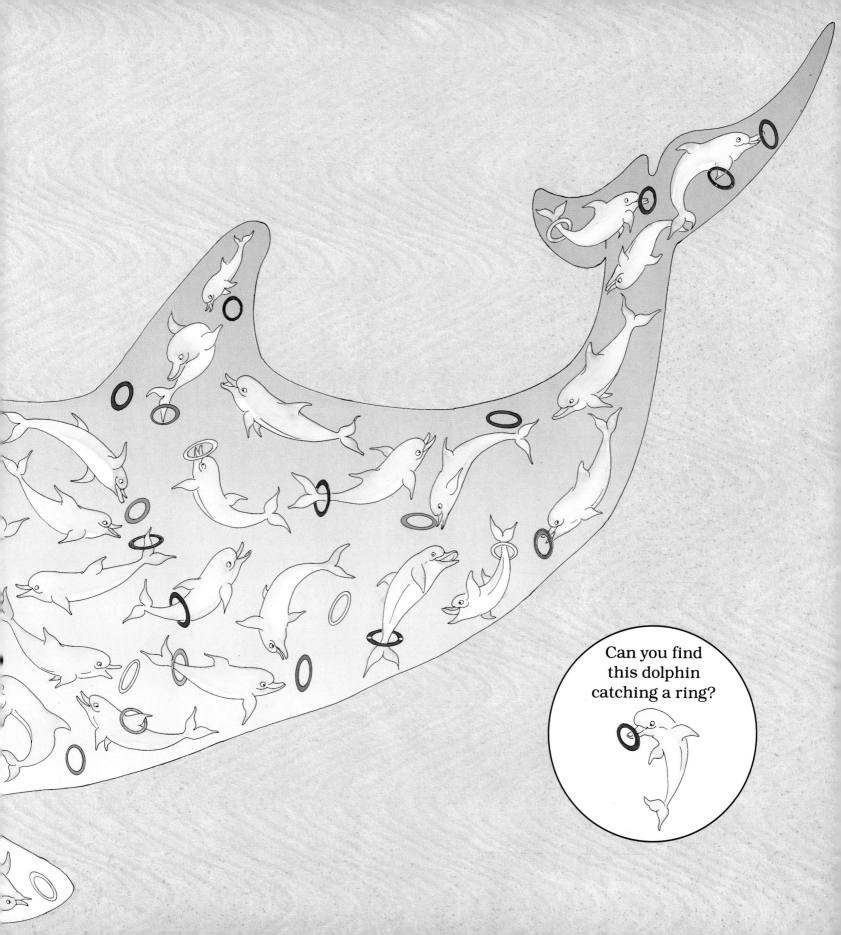

Can you find
this dolphin
catching a ring?

platypus

Can you find this platypus pup?

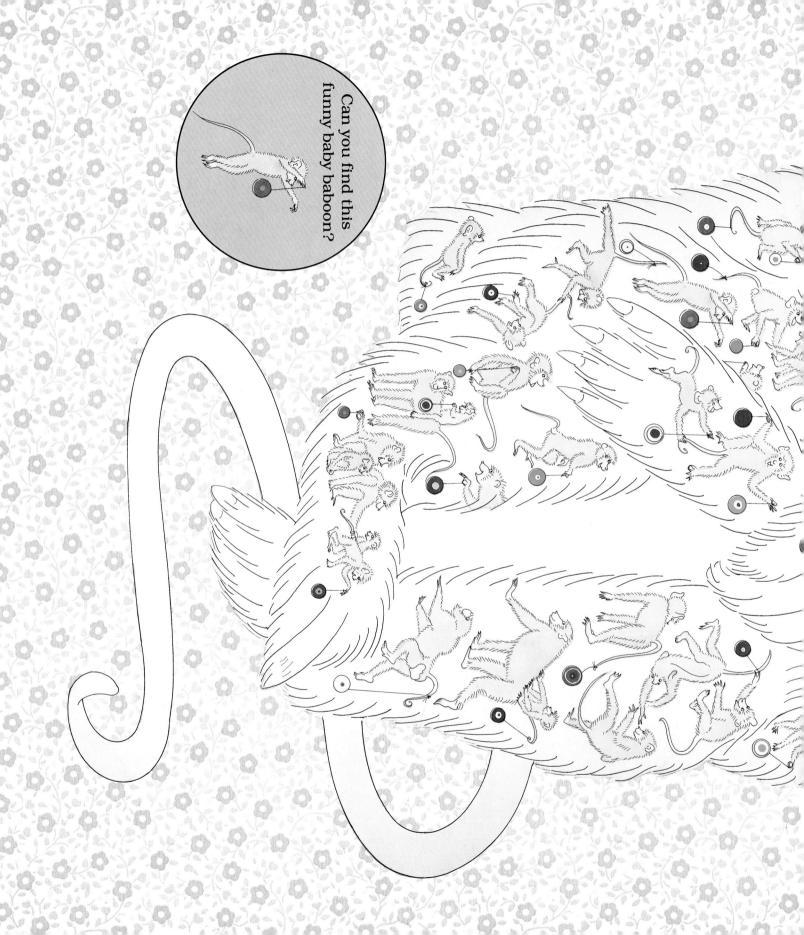

Can you find this funny baby baboon?

baboon

elephant

Can you find this playful elephant?

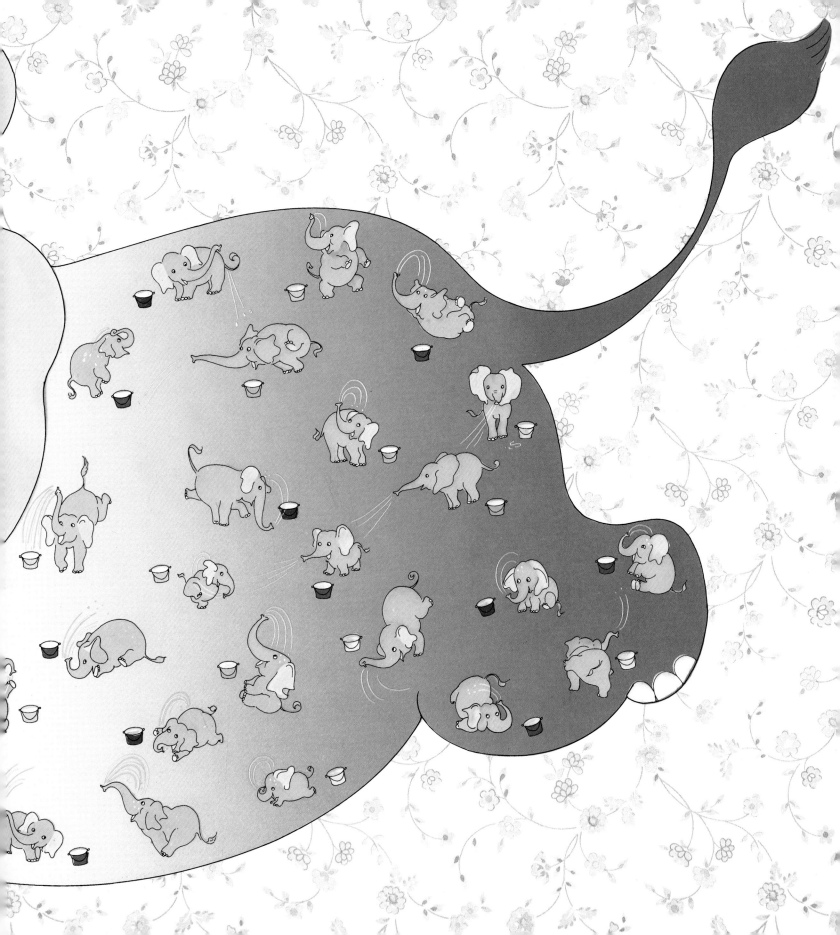

puppy

Can you find
this puppy
chewing a bone?

kittens

Can you find this sleepy kitten?

llama

Can you find this little llama?

deer

Can you find this prancing fawn?

Can you find this
furry squirrel?

squirrel

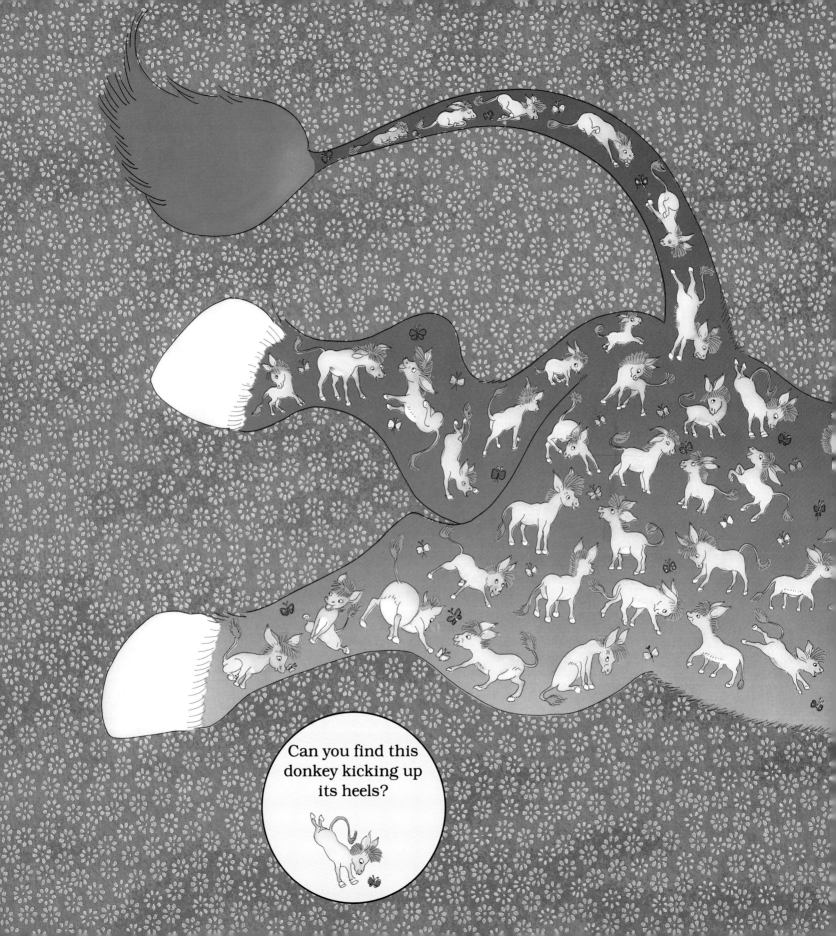

Can you find this
donkey kicking up
its heels?

donkey

seal

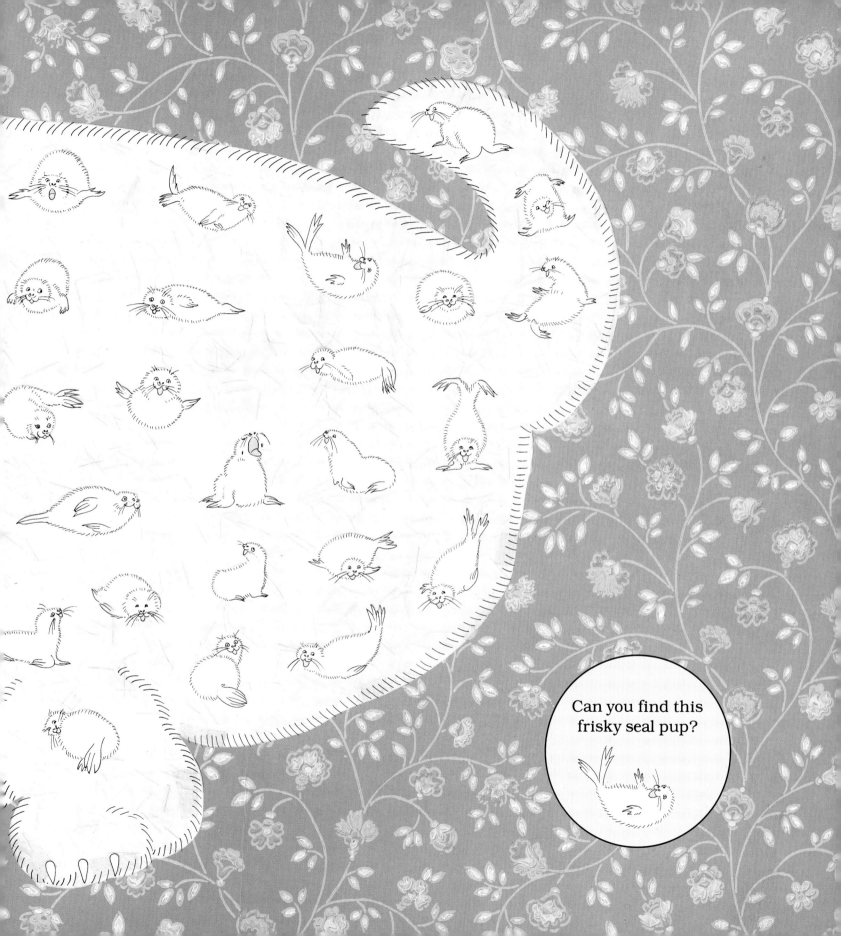

Can you find this
frisky seal pup?